D1141088

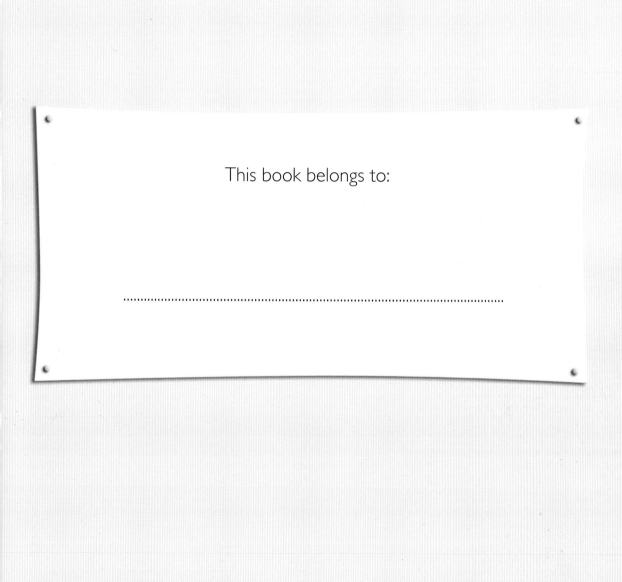

This book belongs to:

....

Bob the Builder
Story Treasury

A treasury of 12 favourite stories from the
Bob the Builder Story Library Collection

Bob the Builder
Story Treasury

With 12 favourite stories

EGMONT

EGMONT

We bring stories to life

First published in Great Britain in 2008
by Egmont UK Limited
239 Kensington High Street
London W8 6SA

Illustrations by Craig Cameron, Dynamo, Pulsar, Jerry Smith and Jorge Santillan

HIT entertainment

Printed in Dubai

978 1 4052 4267 7
1 3 5 7 9 10 8 6 4 2

Contents

Bob is a builder who lives in Sunflower Valley. With help from his team, he can turn his hand to building anything!

Dizzy the cement mixer is just like her name! Fun and excitable, she loves her job and is always the first team member to say 'yes' to a job – no matter what!

Muck's a digger who loves his job! Never afraid of hard work, he can act first and think later, but he always puts things right in the end.

Benny the little digger loves getting the job done! Bright and enthusiastic, he looks up to Scoop and enjoys learning the job from him.

Travis the tractor works for Farmer Pickles, but Travis is always happy to help Bob's team. He also keeps an eye on Spud.

Lofty the crane is very strong and tall, but is also rather shy. Bob's team make sure he's included, and he always makes the best of a job!

Scrambler is a four-wheel-drive vehicle with a trailer, who helps by driving Bob and his materials around. Life is one long adventure to him!

Wendy is Bob's business partner. She always has good ideas, and often has to remind Bob to do things – like turning on his mobile phone!

Sumsy the forklift truck is part of Farmer Pickles' team. She loves to count and is a brilliant help to Bob, too.

Roley is a very dependable member of the team. He slowly and steadily smooths out tarmac – and problems! His best friend is Bird.

Scoop is a digger, and the unspoken leader of Bob's team. He loves solving problems, and often plays practical jokes!

Spud is Farmer Pickles' scarecrow. Much to Farmer Pickles' annoyance, Spud prefers spending time with Bob's team rather than scaring birds!

Bob
and the Big Plan

When Bob hears about a
competition to build a new town in Sunflower Valley,
he faces his biggest building challenge yet.
He's going to need a Big Plan . . .

Bob and the team were busy at work, building a bigger office for Mr Adams the architect.

"I'll need more space if I win the competition to plan a new town in Sunflower Valley," Mr Adams explained. "I've been working on my model for weeks!"

"We used to go to Sunflower Valley on holiday when I was young!" said Bob.

But Bob felt sad when he saw the model. Mr Adams had turned Sunflower Valley into a noisy city, packed with busy roads and big buildings.

"I'm taking this to the town hall, so everyone can have a good look," said Mr Adams. "The judging is the day after tomorrow. Goodbye, Bob!"

"Why don't you enter the competition, Bob?" asked Muck, later on.

"Great idea!" said Dizzy.

"Ho, ho! I'm a builder, not an architect like Mr Adams," said Bob. "And I have lots of work to do here."

Dizzy and Muck were disappointed. But the next morning, Bob changed his mind. He didn't want Sunflower Valley to be spoiled.

"What about the job here, Bob?" asked Scoop, sounding worried.

"Can you finish the foundations by yourselves?" said Bob. "The competition is tomorrow!"

"Can we build it?" said Scoop.

"Yes, we can!" chimed Roley and Muck.

"Er, yeah, I think so," added Lofty.

Back at the yard, Bob was looking through his books
for ideas.

"Wow! Look at these buildings, Pilchard," said Bob.
"I'll need a Big Plan to win this competition!"

"Miaow!" said Pilchard.

Later, Roley, Pilchard and Bird were watching Bob sketch his ideas for Sunflower Valley. But when Bob drew houses, they didn't look right.

"Toot, toot!" squawked Bird. He was showing Bob his nest.

"Good idea, Bird!" smiled Bob. "I'll have houses that don't spoil the countryside, like yours!"

"Brilliant!" said Roley.

Bob had almost finished his model, when he heard a noise outside. Vrrooom! Vrrooom!

Just then, Mr Bentley appeared on a shiny off-road vehicle.

"Hello, Bob," he said. "I'm just taking Scrambler to the town hall – he's part of the prize for the competition!"

"Nice to meet you, Scrambler!" smiled Bob.

At Mr Adams' office, the team was in trouble. Dizzy was pouring out cement for the foundations, when Scoop noticed the markers were in the wrong place. Concrete spilled everywhere!

"Oh, no! What are we going to do?" worried Scoop.

"We'll have to fetch Bob before the concrete goes hard!" said Muck.

"We're really sorry, Bob," said Muck, when Bob arrived. "We made a mistake!"

"Now you won't have time to finish your model," sighed Dizzy.

"If we work quickly, we can move the concrete before it sets and use it later," said Bob, kindly.

"Reduce, reuse, recycle!" said the team. And they worked together until the job was done.

Bob had just arrived back in the yard when, suddenly, the lights went out.

"It's a power cut!" said Bob. "Fetch some lamps, Muck." While Bob finished his model, he told the machines about the different ways to make power. "We'll use the sun and the wind to power Sunflower Valley!" he said.

"Wind turbines and solar panels! How cool!" said Scoop, with excitement.

The next day at the town hall, Mr Adams was finishing his speech when Bob appeared.

"Wait!" shouted Bob. "Here's my Big Plan for Sunflower Valley! We'd use recycled things to build a beautiful town," he explained. "Everything would be powered by water, wind and sun to save energy!"

"Ooh!" and "Wow!" went the crowd, when they saw Bob's model.

The judges looked at both models and nodded their heads.

"It gives me great pleasure to declare the winner and present him with Scrambler. It's . . . Bob the Builder!" said the Mayoress.

"We hope you'll plan and build Sunflower Valley!" said a judge.

Bob was very happy. "Welcome to the team, Scrambler!" he smiled.

"Sunflower Valley, here we come!" cheered Scrambler.

Dizzy
and the Talkie-Talkie

When Wendy brings the talkie-talkies
to Sunflower Valley the machines have
lots of fun with them.
But Dizzy soon finds out how helpful
they can be . . .

One sunny morning, Bob and the team were gathered around a large metal tank in the new yard in Sunflower Valley.

"This will be our new water tank," Bob told the machines. "We can use it to store our water. We will pump the water from the ground through the pipes using a hand pump."

"Hello, everyone!" called Wendy, driving into the yard on Scrambler.

"I've got a present for each of you. They're called talkie-talkies! You can use the headsets to talk to each other wherever you are in Sunflower Valley!" said Wendy, as she handed out the headsets.

"Rock and roll!" smiled Roley.

"That reminds me," said Bob. "We still need some rocks for the tank."

"Dizzy and I can go and find rocks," suggested Scrambler. "We can use the talkie-talkies to let Muck know when we find some. Let's scram!"

"Remember your way so you can get back," called Wendy as they left.

"OK, team? Can we build it?" Bob asked.

"Yes, we can!" everyone cheered.

"Then let's get started! Lofty, you will be getting soil out using this special drill so we can reach the water."

"OK, Bob," said Lofty, and he got to work.

"Dizzy to Scrambler! Can you hear me?" asked Dizzy.
The friends were having fun using the talkie-talkies!
"Cor, look at that big boulder," said Scrambler.
"We won't forget we passed that!"
Dizzy and Scrambler came to a sudden stop.
There had been a landslide and the path was
blocked with rocks!

Dizzy called Muck to tell him they had found some rocks.

Muck set off down the track that Dizzy and Scrambler had taken.

Very soon, Muck came to the big boulder. "Muck to Dizzy, which way do I go at the big boulder, please?" he asked, using his talkie-talkie.

"Erm, you turn left," Dizzy told Muck.

Muck carried on until he came to two trees that looked like an arch. Dizzy couldn't remember seeing an arch.

"Go right, I think," said Dizzy.

"And where do I go at the woods?" asked Muck.

"Erm, I don't remember any woods," replied Dizzy.

"Oh, no!" cried Muck. "I'm lost!"

Dizzy had an idea. "What can you see around you?" she asked Muck.

"Erm, a big hill with a cloud on top," replied Muck.

"Cool as a mule, Muck! Coz I see the big hill with the cloud, too," added Scrambler, over his talkie-talkie. "Head for the hill and you should find us."

Dizzy and Scrambler were starting to wonder if Muck would ever find them when Muck appeared suddenly.

"Muck's on the job!" he grinned. "Let's load up those rocks and get them back to Bob."

"But we don't know how to get back," moaned Scrambler.

Dizzy remembered how Muck had found them.

"Dizzy to Roley," she whispered into the talkie-talkie. "What big things can you see?"

"A really tall tree, taller than all the others," Roley whispered quietly back.

"Come on!" Dizzy told Roley and Muck. "Let's head for the really tall tree!"

Back at the yard, Bob was beginning to wonder where Dizzy, Scrambler and Muck had got to.

"Call them on the talkie-talkie base unit!" suggested Wendy.

"Bob to Dizzy!" Bob began.

"Dizzy to Bob!" came a voice right behind him. "We're back! And we've got rocks."

Soon the water tank was finished. Wendy tried the pump and the pipes began to rattle.

Splash! Water flew out of the pipes and soaked poor Bob!

"Dizzy to Bob," giggled Dizzy. "Hee, hee, you left the tap on!"

"Oh, Dizzy!" said Bob.

And everybody began to laugh! It was another job well done for Bob and the machine team.

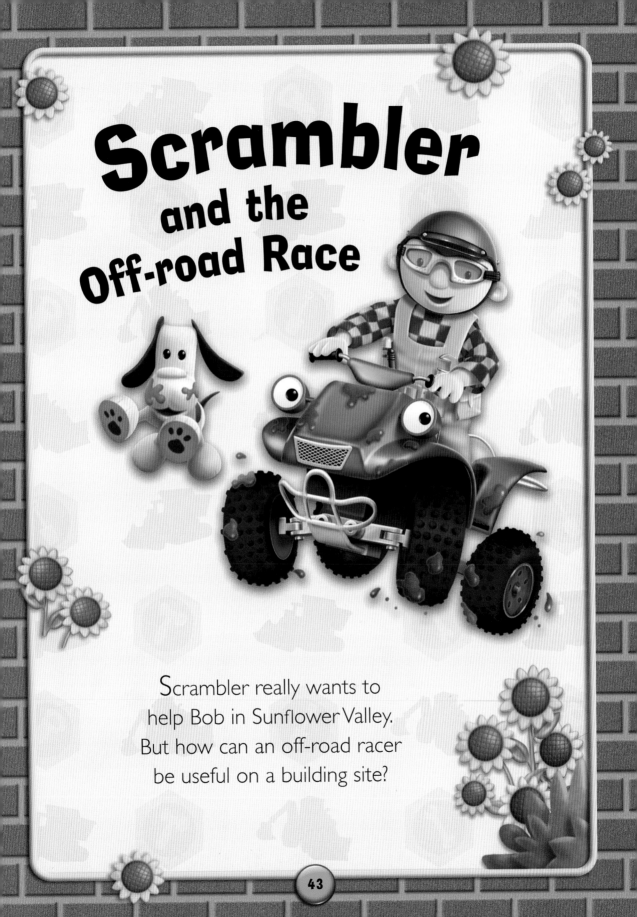

Scrambler
and the
Off-road Race

Scrambler really wants to
help Bob in Sunflower Valley.
But how can an off-road racer
be useful on a building site?

It was a lovely day in Sunflower Valley, and the team had a new job.

"We're building a barn for Farmer Pickles!" announced Bob.

Scruffty was excited. "Ruff! Ruff!" he barked, as he raced around Bob's legs.

But Bob didn't have time to play.

Scrambler was excited, too. He really wanted to help Bob and Wendy.

"What will I be doing?" he asked.

Bob shook his head.

"I'm sorry, Scrambler," he said. "But there isn't really a job for you to do."

Scrambler was disappointed. But then Bob had an idea.

"There is something you can do," smiled Bob. "You can take Scruffty for a walk!"

"But that's not a proper job," said Scrambler, sadly.

"Yes it is," replied Bob. "You'll be keeping Scruffty safe."

The whole team was excited about building the barn.

"Can we build it?" Scoop asked.

"Yes, we can!" the machines all cried.

"Er, yeah, I think so," added Lofty.

But poor Scrambler said nothing. He trailed sadly off to walk Scruffty.

Scruffty ran on ahead, panting excitedly. "Ruff! Ruff!"
Scrambler followed slowly. He felt miserable.
   "I can't believe I'm walking a dog!" he grumbled.
"I thought I was going to get something
important to do."

But when they got to the woods, Scrambler found he was starting to have fun with Scruffty. Especially when they played hide-and-seek!

But when it was Scruffty's turn to hide, he ran off instead. The little dog didn't understand how to play the game!

Back at the site, everyone was working very hard.

Lofty was helping Bob and Wendy set up a wooden frame for the walls and roof of the barn.

Dizzy was pouring concrete to make the floor, and Roley was rolling it flat.

Scrambler and Scruffty chased each other until they found themselves in a beautiful valley, full of twisty paths and ditches.

"Wow!" said Scrambler. "Let's have an off-road race!"

"Ruff!" barked Scruffty, running ahead. The race was on!

The team had been busy all morning, and now the outside of the barn was completely finished.

"Excellent!" said Bob. "Now we need to build some shelves for Farmer Pickles to store things on."

"We'll need to concentrate," said Wendy. "It's a good thing Scruffty's not here!"

Scrambler and Scruffty were having the best time ever. They raced over rocks and through streams, getting very mucky.

"RUFF! RUFF! RUFF!" barked Scruffty, running through a hollow log.

"WHEEEEE!" cried Scrambler. "You can't catch me!"

Scruffty landed in a big muddy puddle. Splash!

Back at the barn, work was finished. Bob and Wendy were having a rest and a cup of tea.

"I wonder where Scrambler's got to with Scruffty?" wondered Wendy, looking around.

Just then, Scrambler rumbled up. He was carrying something in his trailer.

"Scruffty's asleep!" said Scrambler. "But I'm not tired."
He tried not to yawn.

"See . . . dog-walking is a proper job," said Bob, lifting
Scruffty from the trailer. "And you made a friend!"

Scruffty woke up and licked his new friend's nose. "Ruff!"

"Making friends is wicked!" Scrambler grinned happily.

Wendy and the Surprise Party

When Wendy planned a surprise party
for Bob, she had to organise the dome
building work at the same time!
Would Wendy be able to do both?

In Sunflower Valley, Bob and the team were building a dome.

"You've done a great job getting all the parts, Wendy," said Bob. "So I think you should be in charge."

"Oh Bob, I'd love to!" replied Wendy. But then she began to look worried.

As Bob walked away, Wendy whispered to the machines: "I need you to help me keep Bob busy. I'm planning a surprise party for him tomorrow night at the dome! Mr Bentley is letting everyone know."

"But the dome isn't built yet!" cried Muck.

Wendy wasn't worried about building the dome. But she was worried about how she was going to organise the party! Bob and the machines were ready to start.

"Can we build it?" asked Scoop.

"Yes, we can!" replied the machines.

"Er . . . yeah, I think so," added Lofty.

They dug the foundations and made a timber frame.

Then Scrambler whizzed in with Mr and Mrs Bentley.

"Hello, everybody!" said Mr Bentley. "We are here to pick a spot for our new house!"

"We're going to live in a tent while we build it," added Mrs Bentley.

"I'll show you where to pitch it," offered Wendy. But she was really leaving so she could organise the party!

Wendy had just picked up her phone when Scoop arrived.

"Can you come back and tell Bob what to do next?" asked Scoop.

"Bernard will help you with the party tonight," said Mrs Bentley.

"Tonight?" replied Wendy. "But the party is tomorrow!"

Mr Bentley had told everyone to come on the wrong night! Wendy decided that she would organise the party when she got back from the building site.

"We've got to be quick or it won't be finished in time," said Wendy, when she saw Bob and Dizzy looking at the dome pieces.

"In time for what?" asked Bob.

"Oh, nothing Bob!" replied Wendy, hurriedly.

Soon the first layer of the dome was complete. Wendy decided to sneak away to make the phone calls about the party.

"Wendy, what do we need to do next?" asked Bob.

"Just look at my notes," called Wendy. "It's all in there!"

And then she zoomed away on Muck, leaving Bob looking confused.

Wendy arrived at her mobile home and found the Bentleys there.

"I'm just calling Mrs Percival," said Mr Bentley.

"Oh, I'll talk to her," said Wendy, nervously.

Just then, Farmer Pickles arrived with everyone from Bobsville, including Mrs Percival! Wendy was worried that Bob might see them.

But Wendy and Muck had to go back to the site.

"You get back to the dome and we'll sort out everything for the party," said Mr Bentley.

"Oh no, I can deal with it," said Wendy. "Don't do anything, Mr Bentley. I will be back soon."

At the site, Wendy soon saw that Bob hadn't left space for the doors into the dome!

"Oops, I'll just have to start this layer again!" said Bob.

"But that will take too long!" said Wendy.

"Wendy, why don't you let Mr Bentley organise the party?" whispered Muck. "You can't organise the dome and the party at the same time."

Just then, Scrambler zoomed in with Mr Bentley.

"Oh, Mr Bentley, I'm sorry I wouldn't let you help," said Wendy. "Can you organise the party?"

"I would be delighted!" replied Mr Bentley, and Scrambler zoomed off!

With the team working together, the dome was soon finished. Bob went to his mobile home to get some cordial to celebrate.

But when he returned, the dome was decorated with balloons and everyone was wearing party hats!

"Surprise!" cried the Bobsvillagers.

"I don't believe it!" said Bob. "Wendy, when did you manage to organise all this?"

"I've had lots of help!" smiled Wendy.

And then everyone cheered, "Hooray for Sunflower Valley!" as fireworks exploded.

Muck and the Machine Convoy

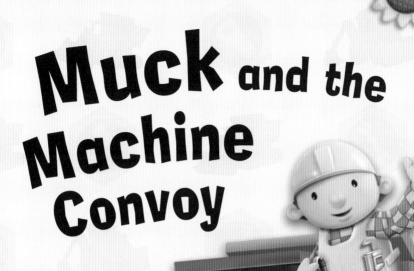

When the Old Watermill needs a new waterwheel,
Muck is given the job of team leader.
But can he lead the machines safely to the mill?

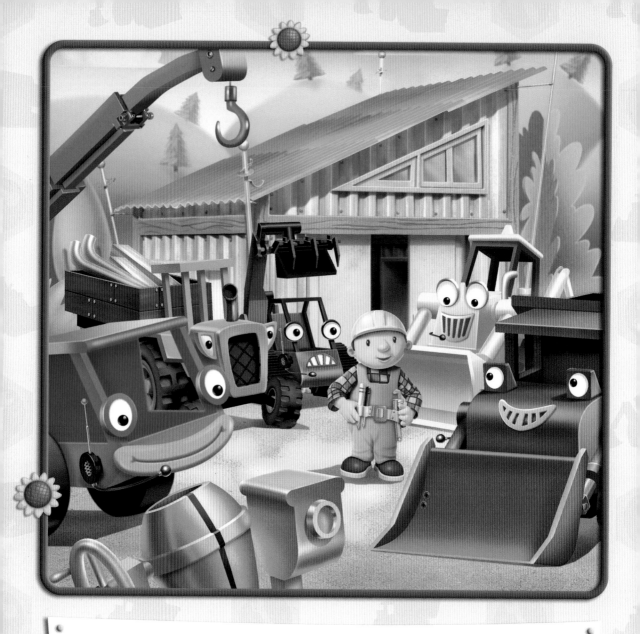

Bob and the team were going to build a waterwheel for the Old Watermill.

"How will it work?" wondered Scoop.

Bob explained that the flow of the river would push the waterwheel round. The wheel would then turn the cogs inside the mill, and the cogs would turn big stones that would rub together and crush the grain into flour.

"Water power! Cool!" said Muck.

"We have to take the waterwheel to the mill," said Bob. "It comes apart, so we can take it in pieces."

Bob climbed up the ladder and loosened some nuts and screws. Lofty carefully put the pieces in Muck's tipper and Scoop's scoop, and the final part on to Benny's forklift. The parts were heavy. It was going to be a bumpy ride!

"Muck, you will be in charge of the convoy," said Bob.

"Erm . . . Bob, what's a convoy?" Muck asked.

"It's when a group of machines follow each other in a line," Bob said. "You will be the leader because you can flatten a path with your caterpillar tracks for the others to follow."

Muck's new job made him feel special. He didn't want to make any mistakes.

Bob told Muck how to get to the Old Watermill.
"But remember," he said, "don't go into the marshland, or you'll get stuck."

"Can Muck lead us?" said Scoop.

"Yes, he can," called the team.

"Er, yeah. I hope so," worried Lofty.

"You can rely on Muck! Convoy – follow me!" said Muck, whizzing ahead. Benny, Scoop and Lofty rolled along behind him.

Bob, Travis and Dizzy took a short cut to take the scaffolding to the mill, where Wendy was waiting.

Meanwhile, the convoy was doing well. On the way they saw a line of ducks waddle across the track.

"Oh, hello, duckies. You're in a convoy just like us!" chuckled Muck.

But there was no time to stop and talk, so Muck and the team hurried on.

Meanwhile, at the Old Watermill, Bob and Wendy had almost finished the scaffolding.

"I wonder what's taking Muck so long?" thought Bob. "I'll call him on the talkie-talkie," he said. "Bob to Muck. How are you doing? Over."

"Umm . . . hello, Bob. We're doing . . . really well," said Muck, quietly.

"Great. See you soon. Out," said Bob.

But Muck and the convoy weren't doing well, at all.
"Are you sure you went the right way, Muck?" asked Lofty.
"Quiet, please. Your leader needs to think!" huffed Muck,
and rolled along bravely. But he was soon feeling glum.
"Oh, no! We're right back where we started!" moaned Benny.
The convoy was back at the yard!

By now, Muck and the convoy were feeling very tired. Finally, they reached the river.

"Well done, Muck! We're nearly there!" cheered Lofty.

"I did it! Let's cut across the marsh. It'll be quicker," said Muck, rolling down the riverbank.

But the convoy didn't follow at once. "I'm sure Muck knows what he's doing," urged Scoop. "Follow the leader!"

Schlup . . . schlup . . . schlup went their wheels through the muddy marsh.

Poor Lofty, his wheels had sunk deep into the mud.

"You said you wouldn't get me stuck, Muck!" he bawled.

"This is all my fault. Leaders shouldn't make mistakes," worried Muck.

The ducklings were crossing the marsh, too. But one was stuck, like Lofty. The mother duck gave it a push, and the duckling waddled free.

Watching the ducks gave Muck an idea. He pushed Lofty with all his might. Slowly, Lofty eased out of the marsh and on to the track.

"Someone else should be leader. I've made too many mistakes," sighed Muck.

"Bob says good leaders are ones who make a mistake and then put it right. And you did just that!" said Scoop, kindly.

The team got back in line, ready for Muck to lead them to the mill.

Finally, Muck's convoy arrived at the mill.

"I'm sorry, Bob," mumbled Muck. "We went in a big circle … and got lost. Then Lofty got stuck in the marsh …"

"Muck did a brilliant job leading us here," said Scoop.

"Yeah, he was like, unreal banana peel!" joined in Benny.

"Well done, Muck," cheered Bob.

Muck beamed happily with everyone's praise.

"Now, let's finish building the waterwheel," said Bob. With all the team helping, it was soon complete. Bob turned the handle outside and the waterwheel began to turn.

"Hooray!" cheered the team.

Just then, the mother duck and her ducklings floated past on the river.

"Looks like we both got our convoys here safely!" Muck said, proudly.

Benny and the Important Job

Bob and the machines are busy with
a big job — they are building a special
house for the Bentleys.
Benny wants to help, but is the job
too big for him?

Early one morning, Benny the little digger zoomed into
Sunflower Valley. The machines were all still fast asleep in
their shelter.

"Hey, everyone! Wake up!" said Benny.

Bob came to the door of his mobile home.
"What's going on?" he yawned.

"There was no work for me in Bobsville today, so I've
come to help!" said Benny.

"OK, team, rise and shine!" said Bob.

Soon, Benny was following Bob and the team to the site. He was very excited.

"We're building a special house for the Bentleys today," said Bob, "inside this hill!"

"Unreal!" smiled Benny.

"That's just brilliant!" giggled Dizzy.

"Who would have thought!" smiled Scoop.

Mr Bentley arrived to help, too.

"Let's start! What am I doing first?" said Benny, excitedly.

"We need to mark out the foundations. Then Scoop and Muck can start digging," Bob told the machines.

"No prob, Bob!" said Scoop.

"Let's get mucky!" added Muck.

Benny wondered what his job would be.

"When the foundations are ready, Roley can level the ground," said Bob.

"Rock and roll!" revved Roley.

"And Dizzy and I will make concrete blocks for the walls," said Bob.

"I know the perfect place to make them," said Dizzy.

Bob and Dizzy rushed away, leaving Benny behind with Mr Bentley.

Benny wanted to help Scoop and Muck, but Mr Bentley was worried. "This is really a job for big diggers, Benny," he said.

"Little diggers can dig big holes too, you know!" said Benny, in a cross voice.

"OK, but it must be ready tomorrow," said Mr Bentley. "A photographer is coming – our house is going to be on the cover of a magazine!"

Benny began to dig, but the ground was so hard that his digger bounced right off!

"Everything needs to be ready for tomorrow, remember!" said Mr Bentley.

Muck and Scoop had finished digging their holes, so they helped Benny with his.

Benny was sad. "That was my big, important job," he sighed.

The next morning, Bob and the machines reached the site.

Lofty and Wendy brought big glass windows for the Bentleys' house.

"Well done, Wendy," said Mr Bentley. "And well done, Lofty, too!"

"The windows are here, the hill's dug . . . now to mix the concrete," said Bob.

"I'll do it!" said Benny.

"Ha, ha! Don't be silly!" laughed Dizzy. "How can a digger mix concrete?"

"Oh," sighed Benny. He looked sad.

There were lots of jobs for the machines to do, but poor Benny was too small or too slow for any of them.

Muck and Scoop went to fetch the concrete blocks.
Roley rolled the ground flat.
Bob fixed a waterproof sheet to the roof of the hill house.
And Wendy and Lofty fitted the windows.

Benny watched them, miserably. "Nobody needs a little digger like me. I'll just go back to Bobsville," he cried.

But just then, Mrs Bentley and Scrambler arrived. His trailer was loaded with plants.

"Wicked house!" smiled Scrambler.

"Now we just need to put these plants in the garden," said Mrs Bentley.

Mr Bentley gasped. "The photographer from the magazine is coming any minute!"

"What are we going to do?" cried Mrs Bentley. "There's so much digging to do!"

Muck and Scoop wanted to help, but they were too big and heavy to dig the ground.

"I'm small enough," said Benny. "It can be my big, important job!"

"Come on then, Benny! Let's get planting!" smiled Mrs Bentley.

Benny had just finished digging when the photographer, David Daley, arrived. "What a gorgeous home!" he said.

"It's all down to Bob's crew ... especially Benny the digger!" smiled Mr Bentley.

"Let's have a picture," said David Daley. "Join in, Benny. Now smile, everyone!"

The biggest smile belonged to Benny, the little digger.

Sumsy and the Sunflower Spill

Farmer Pickles' Sunflower Oil Factory
is almost ready to open! There's just
one more job to do.
Sumsy arrives to help, but will the
factory open on time?

Farmer Pickles was getting ready for the grand opening of his new Sunflower Oil Factory.

"There's just one more job to do," he said. "I need somewhere for all these boxes."

"No problem," smiled Bob. "We'll build you a bottle depot."

"Thanks, Bob," said Farmer Pickles. "Now I've got a surprise for you! Meet . . ."

"Sumsy the forklift! She's going to move the boxes
with the bottles of sunflower oil from the factory to the
storage depot."

"I can pack 'em! I can stack 'em!" smiled Sumsy. "Hi, everyone!"

"Hello, Sumsy," said Bob, Scoop and Travis.

She looked at Travis. "One, two, three boxes. I love counting!"
Sumsy laughed.

"Right!" said Bob. "I'd better get started building this depot." And off he went.

Farmer Pickles and Travis went too, and Scoop and Sumsy were left on their own.

"I'm Scoop!" said Scoop. "I know everything about Sunflower Valley. I'll show you around. Follow me!"

"What about the boxes?" Sumsy worried. But Scoop had rolled away.

The first stop on Scoop's tour was the homestead.
Then he showed Sumsy the workshops and the storerooms.
"We've plenty of time to work," said Scoop.
But Sumsy looked sad. She knew there were lots of
boxes to be moved.
Soon, they reached the site where Bob and the team
were building the bottle depot.

"Hi, Scoop!" smiled Dizzy.

"Hi, everyone," called Scoop. "This is Sumsy! Sumsy, meet Dizzy, Muck and . . . Roley."

"Rock and ro-ho-ole!" said Roley.

"Three machines. Three!" counted Sumsy. "Three boxes is how many I can fit on my forklift. I can pack 'em, I can stack 'em!" she laughed, and raced away.

Just then, Farmer Pickles arrived with a big crate.
"Look what I've got here!" he said. "A bottle-labelling machine."

He pressed a button and labels began to fly out, sticking themselves to Dizzy, Roley and Bob!

"We're not bottles! Ha, ha!" smiled Dizzy.

"What a sticky situation!" said Farmer Pickles. "I hope Sumsy brings those boxes of bottles soon."

Inside the factory, Sumsy was hard at work.
"Coming through! Ten bottles in every box," she said, whizzing past Scoop.

"Wait!" moaned Scoop. "I haven't shown you all the factory yet! How can I tell you things if you keep driving off?"

Sumsy raced away, with Scoop chasing behind.

Scoop caught up with Sumsy and swerved in front of her
to make her stop.

Sumsy screeched to a halt, but it was too late. CRASH!
The boxes flew off her forklift and smashed on the ground.

"Oh, no!" cried Scoop.

Sumsy and Scoop went to look at the mess. The bottles
were broken and oil had spilled everywhere.

Meanwhile, Bob and the team had nearly finished building the bottle depot.

"Well done, team! We're almost ready for your bottles, Farmer Pickles," he said.

"But then we need labels on the bottles," worried Farmer Pickles. "Where's Sumsy?"

"Here she comes!" said Dizzy, as Sumsy trundled sadly towards them.

Farmer Pickles saw the boxes of broken bottles.
"Oh dear!" he gasped.

"I'm sorry, Farmer Pickles," said Sumsy. "I was trying to do
my job, when, erm . . ."

"It was me," said Scoop. "I got in Sumsy's way. I was
showing her around the valley."

When Scoop found out that the bottles all needed labels,
he felt very sorry. "There's not enough time!" he cried.

"Three boxes fit on my forklift, and two fit in your digger," Sumsy said to Scoop, kindly. "We'll work together to get the job done quicker!"

So that's what they did. Before long, all the boxes were safely in the depot and all the bottles had labels.

Bob finished building the depot wall and the factory was ready to open, just in time!

The grand opening was the next day.

"I declare this Sunflower Oil Factory open!" said Farmer Pickles. And he snipped the ribbon in half.

"Hooray for Farmer Pickles!" cheered Bob.

"And hooray for Sumsy and Scoop!" said Farmer Pickles, proudly.

"Ha, ha!" laughed Sumsy. "When we work together, it's as easy as one, two, three!"

Roley and the Woodland Walk

When Roley tries to help his woodland
friends, they get in the way of Bob
and Wendy's work.
Luckily, Roley comes up with a brilliant idea ...

It was a very hot day in Sunflower Valley.

Bob and Wendy were on their way to build workbenches and fit big tools in the workshop.

"We don't need any help, today," said Bob. "So you can all have the day off!"

The machines wanted to keep cool in the shade. So off they all went to the shelter to play 'I Spy'. Except for Roley ...

Roley had set off into Sunflower Valley to look for his friend, Birdie.

"Birdie," called Roley. "It's your friend, Roley. Birdie! Where are you?"

Roley came to a pond in the clearing, but the hot weather had dried up all the water. Next to the pond, he saw Birdie, looking sad. Roley didn't know what was wrong.

"You're not whistling," worried Roley. "Are you too hot?"

Birdie chirped weakly. Roley wondered how he could help. "Maybe I could find you somewhere to keep cool?"

Just then, Birdie's chicks flew on to Roley's cab. As Roley set off to find some shade, a squirrel hopped out of the trees. He was hot, too.

"Don't worry," said Roley, kindly. "I'll come back for you."

Roley gave Birdie and her chicks a ride to the storeroom. When they arrived, they flew off his cab and headed for the workshop.

"No, no! Not in there. That's where Bob and Wendy are working," he said, and guided them into the cool storeroom.

Then Roley set off to fetch the squirrel.

Wendy and Bob were building a new cupboard to keep all the tools tidy.

They went to the storeroom to get the first big tool – the saw.

They didn't see Birdie and her chicks nestling under the cover!

Roley zoomed back to the clearing. "It's all right, little squirrel," said Roley. "I've got a lovely place for you out of the sun."

Suddenly, three more squirrels scampered down the trees. "Climb aboard," smiled Roley.

Just as he was about to leave, a family of otters dashed out of the bushes. They were hot and thirsty, too.

"Stay here. I'll be right back!" said Roley.

Roley dropped the squirrels off at the storeroom, and then went to fetch the otters.

With the tool cupboard finished, Wendy and Bob wanted to fit the big saw. But when Wendy found the instructions, they were full of holes!

"Oh, no! We can't read this," said Wendy. "Something's been pecking at them!"

Bob and Wendy couldn't fit the saw without the instructions. They decided to fit the next big tool instead – the drill.

As Wendy pulled off the cover, the squirrels scurried away to hide.

"Look, Wendy!" cried Bob. "These instructions are torn, too." They were really puzzled now!

Roley brought the otters to the storeroom and looked around inside.

"Little squirrel . . . Birdie?" he called. "Are you still in there?"

But they weren't! All the animals were in the workshop.

Roley didn't want Bob to see the animals, so he thought of a plan. "I found Birdie. Um . . . she's not well. She needs our help!" he told Bob, making his story up.

Roley took Bob to the dried-up pond.

"Birdie must be thirsty!" said Bob. "When ponds dry up, birds and animals can't get any water. The best way to help is to put some out for them."

Then Bob poured water from his flask. "Now when Birdie comes back, she can have a drink."

Then Bob and Roley rolled back to the workshop.

Back at the workshop, Wendy had some news for them.

"Bob!" she called. "I know why everything was chewed and pecked! The workshop was full of animals! I gave them some water and they've all gone away happy."

Roley felt bad, so he told Bob what had happened.

"Don't worry, Roley," said Bob. "You were only trying to help."

Suddenly, Roley had a brilliant idea . . .

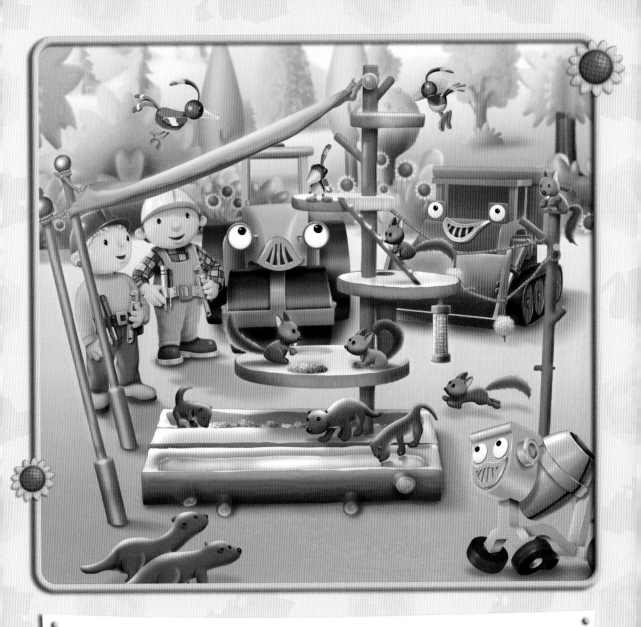

Roley asked the other machines to help gather up old bits of wood so Bob and Wendy could build a bird table. That way, his woodland friends would have food and water, and he would see them all the time.

The team worked together and soon the bird table was finished. "Rock and roll!" smiled Roley.

And now, whenever the animals get thirsty or hot, they visit Roley's bird table.

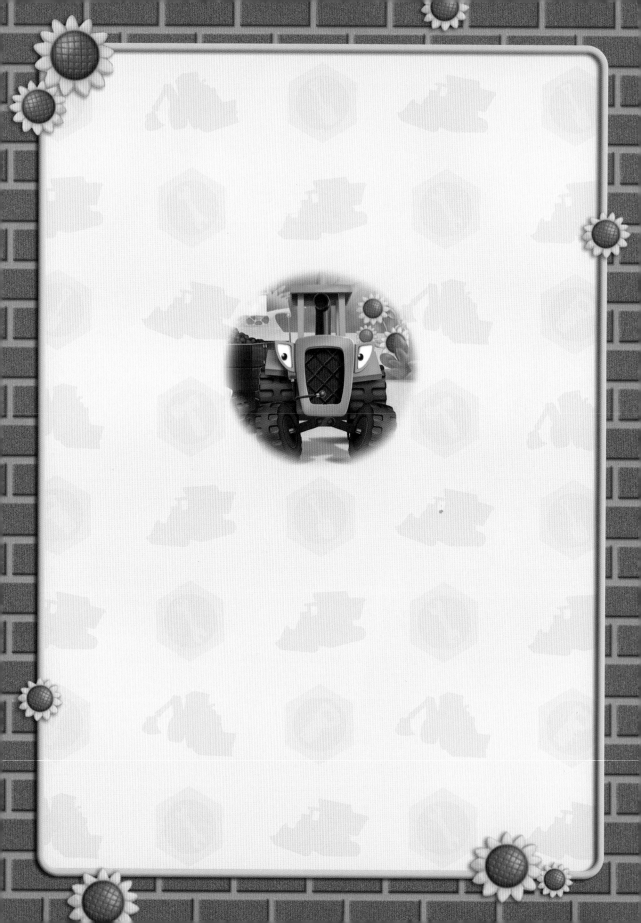

Travis and the Tropical Fruit

When Mr Beasley says he wants
to grow pineapples in Sunflower
Valley, Travis offers to help.
But things go wrong, and Travis and
Spud make a real stink!

Travis the tractor had come to visit his friends in Sunflower Valley.

"Farmer Pickles has gone to Bobsville today," said Travis. "Got any jobs for me?"

"No, sorry, Travis," said Scoop. "But there'll be a job somewhere! You just have to look for it!"

Meanwhile, Mr Beasley was showing a special box to Bob and Wendy.

"My pineapple seedlings have just been delivered!" he smiled, opening the box.

Bob and Wendy were puzzled.

"Sunflower Valley's not hot enough to grow pineapples!" said Bob. "They grow in tropical weather!"

"But the box says they need planting straight away!"
Mr Beasley frowned.

"Don't worry," said Wendy, kindly. "Let's look up pineapples
on the Internet."

Wendy found a picture of a pineapple pit on her
computer and showed Mr Beasley.

"I've never built one of those!" laughed Bob. "It looks like
your pineapples are going to be heated by horse manure!"

Bob went to the yard to tell the team.

"What's horse manure?" asked Muck.

"It's, erm, horse poo," said Bob. "It sounds silly, but it will heat up the pineapples and make them grow!"

"I moved a whole load of horse manure at Farmer Pickles' farm yesterday," said Travis. "I'll fetch it and be back before you know it!"

The farm was far away in Bobsville, but Travis got there
quickly. He loaded up his trailer with the horse manure.
Just then, his talkie-talkie began to crackle. It was Bob!

"Take your time, Travis," said Bob. "The pineapple
pit isn't built yet ... and manure is a bit smelly!"

"Ha, ha! Erm, OK, Bob," said Travis.

132

Travis decided to unload the manure in a clearing by the Bentleys' eco house, until Bob needed it.

Near by, the Bentleys and the Sabatinis were having a picnic.

"Goodness me! Whatever's that smell?" said Mr Bentley. "We can't stay here. Quick, pack up the picnic!"

"Oh, deary me!" worried Travis, and he trundled away with the trailer of manure.

The next day, Mr Beasley went to see how Bob and the team were getting on. They had been very busy building the pineapple pit.

"When we put the manure in, it will heat up the soil and make the seedlings grow!" Bob told Mr Beasley.

"These glass covers will keep them warm and the pong inside!" Wendy laughed.

Travis had taken his trailer to Scarecrow Cottage. He needed Spud to help him move the manure.

"My parsnip nose! What a whiff!" said Spud. He disappeared inside the cottage and came back wearing a funny mask.

"Ta da! Spud's wearing Farmer Pickles' special mask for cleaning out the pig sties!" boomed Spud, through his mask.

Soon, Spud and Travis had made a plan.

"The big pile of manure makes a big stink, but lots of little piles will just make lots of little stinks," said Spud.

"No one'll notice a thing!" agreed Travis.

So Spud shovelled the manure into sacks, then Travis took them away to hide all over Sunflower Valley.

A few days later, it was time to add the manure to the pineapple pits.

Travis and Spud told Bob about how they had stored it in the sacks. "We hid them all over Sunflower Valley," said Spud.

"Oh, dear!" chuckled Bob. "How will we find them again?"

Just then, Mr Bentley arrived. "Don't worry," he said. "I'll soon sniff them out!"

And that's just what they did! Spud, Travis and Mr Bentley searched behind bushes, trees and buildings until they had found all the sacks.

"Wow!" said Travis. "What a clever nose you have, Mr Bentley!"

They took the sacks to Bob, and he and Spud shovelled the manure into the pits.

Before long, the pineapple pits were as hot as a tropical jungle!

Months passed while the pineapples grew, until finally they were ready to eat.

Mr Beasley invited everyone to taste the tropical treat, and it was delicious!

"Horse manure! That's the secret," he laughed. "I'm going to grow all sorts of tropical fruit next – mangoes, bananas ..."

"Oh, no! You know what that means, Travis," groaned Bob. "More manure!"

Lofty
and the
Singing Stars

Farmer Pickles' pickers teach
Lofty to sing. But how can Lofty
be the star of the campfire
sing-along if he has no time
to practise?

One hot summer's day in Sunflower Valley, Bob and Farmer Pickles had a new job for the machines.

"Today, team," said Bob, "we're going to build a bunk house."

"It's a wooden house for my guests to sleep in. Here they come now!" said Farmer Pickles.

Just then, Travis arrived, with three people sitting in his trailer. Lofty followed behind.

The people in the trailer were singing, and before long, Lofty joined in, too:

"... *But the thing that I love pickin',*
– I could pick a ton or two –
Is a great big field of sunflowers,
Every picker knows it's true!"

The machines looked at Lofty, amazed.

"Wow," said Roley, "we've never heard you sing before, Lofty. You're great!"

"Meet Mickey, Vicky and Ricky!" said Lofty, rolling up beside the trailer. "They're the pickers helping with the sunflower harvest. And they're great singers, too!"

The pickers began to sing again.

Lofty smiled. "They've been teaching me songs all morning!" he said.

"Well, you can teach us a song or two while we work," laughed Bob.

The machines sorted the logs for the bunk house, while the pickers prepared to set off to the fields.

"... *Lift the logs and lay them down, All day long!*" sang Lofty.

"You're doing a grand job, Lofty," said Vicky. "Will you be the star of our sing-along around the campfire tonight?"

Lofty was surprised. "Me, the star?" he said. "Oh, er, thanks very much ..."

Suddenly, Lofty didn't feel like singing any more.
Dizzy saw that he looked sad.

"Cheer up, Lofty," said Dizzy. "You're going to be the star!"

"I do like singing, but not on my own. What if I'm no
good?" Lofty worried.

Dizzy smiled, kindly. "You just need to practise. Ha-ha-ha,
I'll help!" She twirled around on the spot. "Let's go and find
somewhere quiet."

Dizzy sped off, but before Lofty could follow, Bob and Wendy called him over.

"Come on, Lofty," said Bob. "Time to get the walls of this bunk house up!"

"We can't do it without you," said Wendy.

Lofty rolled sadly towards the pile of logs. He couldn't practise his singing now. Poor Lofty felt very worried indeed.

Just then, Lofty's talkie-talkie crackled. It was Dizzy. "I'm at Mr Beasley's yurt!" she said. "It's nice and quiet, come quickly!"

So Lofty put down his logs and raced off before anybody noticed.

"I wish I were the star!" said Dizzy, when Lofty arrived. "OK, let's get singing …"

But before Lofty had sung a note, his talkie-talkie crackled again. It was Bob calling him back to the bunk house.

So Lofty trundled back to see Bob. "I'll never be the star if I don't practise," he worried.

"There you are, Lofty!" said Bob. "We can't build this roof without your help."

Lofty lifted the wood for Wendy, while Bob hammered on the roof.

"We'll soon have this job finished," smiled Bob. "Then it'll be sing-along time around the campfire!"

Dizzy called Lofty on his talkie-talkie. She'd found another quiet place.

Lofty crept away again to meet Dizzy, who was hiding by some tall sunflowers. "No one will disturb us here!" she said.

But, just then, the pickers appeared through the sunflowers. "Looking forward to tonight, Lofty?" smiled Mickey.

Before Lofty could answer, Wendy was calling him back to the bunk house.

"We'll never get the job done if you keep disappearing!" laughed Wendy, when Lofty arrived back at the bunk house.

"We wouldn't want to miss the sing-along," added Scoop. "You're the star, after all!"

Lofty said nothing. Bob, Wendy and the machines worked quickly to fit the bunks into place. Soon, the work was done.

"We did it!" cheered Bob. "Now for some singing fun."

As the sun set, everyone gathered around the finished bunk house. Lofty looked very worried.

"Hi, Lofty!" said Mickey. "Are you excited?"

"Not really," cried Lofty. "I'm scared. I don't want to be the star and sing on my own."

Mickey smiled. "Oh, Lofty," he said, "you don't have to sing on your own!"

Lofty was puzzled. "I don't?" he said.

"We sing songs about who we meet," said Ricky. "Tonight's song is all about you."

Lofty had been worrying for nothing all day! Now he was excited about the song.

The pickers started to sing:

"We all said to Bob, pick Lofty for the job!"

"Next time you're worried about something, Lofty, talk to us," said Bob.

"I will," Lofty laughed. "I'm Lofty the star!"

Scoop and the Bakery Build Build

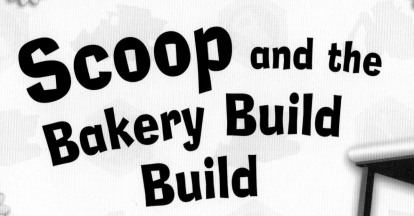

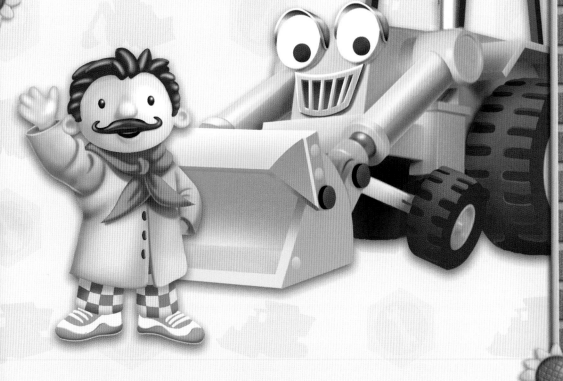

The team has a big job – they're
building a bakery! Scoop is in charge
of showing Benny what to do,
but will the big digger make
a good teacher?

One morning in the New Yard, Bob was checking he had all he needed in Travis' trailer. Dizzy, Scoop and Lofty wondered what he was up to.

"This is a flat-packed bakery – it comes in pieces!" said Bob. "We're going to put it together for Mr Sabatini, by the river."

"Coooool!" said Scoop.

"And," said Bob, "there's a surprise for you when we get there, Scoop!"

Bob and the machines made their way to the riverbank. Scoop was very excited. "So where's my surprise, Bob?" he asked.

At that moment, Benny rolled out from behind a bush. "Hi, Big Banana!" he laughed.

Scoop jumped. So that was his surprise!

"Scoop," said Bob, "we thought it would be a good idea if Benny joined you on this job and learned a few tips."

Scoop looked confused. "You need a digger to teach a digger?"

Bob smiled. "Who better to teach Benny than the biggest and best digger I know?"

Scoop felt happy. Then he whispered to Bob, "Are you sure I can do it?"

"Of course you can!" said Bob. "Now, let's get this lot unloaded. Can we build it?"

"Yes, we can!" cheered the machines.

"Er, yeah . . . I think so," added Lofty.

Bob marked out the foundations, while Scoop told Benny what to do.

Suddenly, Spud appeared. "Ooh, what's going on here?" he asked.

"I'm teaching Benny how to make the foundations for Mr Sabatini's bakery," said Scoop, proudly.

Spud rubbed his tummy. "A bakery? That means yummy bread. I love bread, I do . . . can I help too, Bob?"

Bob laughed. "Sorry, Spud, I think we've got all the help we need today," he said.

Spud looked very sorry for himself.

Bob's next job was to collect the bakery's oven with Lofty and Travis.

"It's a clever oven heated by burning these special briquettes," he said. "And we make the briquettes from pressed sunflower stalks with this machine. Look!"

Bob showed them all how it worked before setting off to fetch the oven.

When Bob had gone, Spud pleaded with Scoop to let him help. "Please! I'll do anything!"

So Scoop said that Spud could make the briquettes.

"Great idea!" smiled Spud. He was looking forward to trying some tasty bread, and skipped off with the briquette machine.

Meanwhile, Scoop and Benny began to dig the bakery's foundations.

"OK, Benny, make sure you dig inside the area marked by Bob!" said Scoop.

Before long, the digging was done and Dizzy filled the area with concrete.

"What's next, Scoop?" asked Benny, eagerly.

Scoop wasn't sure, so Dizzy said they should wait for Bob.

Benny looked disappointed. "But you can do anything, can't you, Scoop?"

"Well …" Scoop said, looking flustered, "we could put up the framework."

Dizzy was worried. "You've never done that without Bob," she warned.

But Scoop said he'd watched it being done lots of times. "And Benny's got to learn somehow!" he added.

So the two diggers got to work.

"Wow! You know your stuff!" Benny grinned, when the framework was in place. "What's next? The roof?"

"Well, I suppose we could ..." said Scoop.

"We should wait for Bob!" Dizzy huffed.

Scoop didn't listen and lifted up the roof. But the framework wasn't strong enough and the roof began to wobble! Scoop hurried underneath to support it ... but his wheels sank into the wet concrete!

Benny and Dizzy rushed off to find help. Moments later, Bob, Lofty and Travis arrived – just in time to rescue Scoop.

"I'm sorry, Bob," cried Scoop. "All I've taught Benny is how to make mistakes!"

"Oh, Scoop," said Bob, kindly. "We all need help sometimes. And you've taught yourself a good lesson today!"

"Yes! Next time, I won't try to do things all by myself," Scoop promised.

"Ok!" said Bob. "We've a bakery to finish! Can we build it?"

"Yes, we can!" called the machines.

"Er, yeah . . . I think so," added Lofty.

They all set to work, levelling the concrete and fixing the framework, roof and walls.

Mr and Mrs Sabatini arrived, just as the special oven was being wheeled inside. "It's magnificent!" they said happily. "Thank you so much, everyone!"

Just then, Bob remembered something. "We forgot to make the briquettes for the oven!" he cried.

"It's OK, I asked Spud to do it!" said Scoop.

"Phew!" smiled Bob. "What would I do without you, Scoop?"

Later, Mr Sabatini baked the very first loaf of bread. It was shaped just like Scoop!

"Ha, ha! Scoop," drooled Spud. "You're the tastiest digger in Sunflower Valley!"

Spud and the Funny Trees

Spud is too noisy and Farmer
Pickles has had enough!
How can Spud keep quiet and
be helpful at the same time?

It was night-time in Sunflower Valley and everybody was in bed. At Scarecrow Cottage, Spud was snoring loudly. Poor Farmer Pickles couldn't sleep!

He sat up in bed, and rubbed his eyes. Then he lay down again wearily and put his pillow over his ears.

Spud's snoring was so loud that Scruffty could hear it too — from his kennel, outside!

"Ruff, ruff," whined Scruffty.

At the yard the next morning, Bob told the machines
what they were going to do that day.

"We're using these logs to build a safety fence on the
riverbank beside Mr Sabatini's windmill," he said.

"A safety fence?" rumbled Roley. "Why?"

Bob laughed. "To stop people from falling into the river,
of course!" he said.

Soon, Wendy arrived, wearing a lifebelt around her waist. Lofty looked puzzled.

"It's a lifebelt, Lofty," explained Wendy. "You throw it to people if they fall into water and it helps them stay afloat!"

"We're going to hang it next to the safety fence," added Bob.

"Well, I'd better be off to the factory." said Wendy, waving goodbye. "I promised to help Farmer Pickles with a big delivery."

At the Sunflower Oil factory, Farmer Pickles was so tired after his noisy night that he arrived very late with his delivery of sunflowers.

"Sorry, I didn't get a wink of sleep last night," he yawned. "Spud is just too noisy! I'm going to have to ask him to move."

Farmer Pickles didn't see that Spud and Scruffty were peeping round the door.

Spud was shocked! "Did you hear that, Scruffty?" he asked. "Farmer Pickles wants me to leave Scarecrow Cottage because I'm too noisy!"

Spud stomped off, crossly. "We'll soon see about that," he said.

As he thudded through the woods, some rabbits hopped across his path.

"Hmm," he wondered. "Rabbits have quiet paws. I wish my feet could be so quiet ..."

Spud sat down beside some cork trees. He picked up a piece of bark.

"This is nice and soft," he said to himself. "It must have fallen off this funny tree."

He looked closely at the tree trunk. "Aha! Spuddie's got an idea!"

Spud began collecting bark from the cork trees. Soon, he had made himself a pair of special cork shoes. "Now I'm as quiet as a rabbit!" he said, tiptoeing on his way.

Meanwhile, on the riverbank, the new safety fence was taking shape.

"Can we build it?" called Bob.

"Yes, we can!" piped the machines.

"Er, yeah . . . I think so," added Lofty.

They didn't notice Spud creeping up behind them in his new, quiet shoes.

Bob had just picked up the lifebelt to hang in its new home, when suddenly Spud tapped him on the shoulder.

"Ta-da!" exclaimed Spud, smiling.

Bob was so surprised that he dropped the lifebelt, which rolled towards Lofty, who was reversing.

"Look out!" cried Bob. But it was too late. Lofty had crushed it.

"Sorry, Bob!" said Spud. "I was just trying to be Silent Spud because Farmer Pickles says I'm too noisy."

Spud showed Bob his quiet shoes.

Bob chuckled. Then he looked closely at Spud's shoes.
"Cork! Of course!" said Bob. He had an idea.
"Let's go and find those cork trees, Muck," he said.
"I think they might solve our problem!"
Sure enough, when they reached the wood, Bob
found that the bark from the cork trees was light
and strong — just right to make a new lifebelt.

Back at the factory, all the bottles of oil were loaded into crates, ready for delivery. There were just enough bottle tops for the bottles.

Travis and Farmer Pickles hadn't gone far when suddenly Spud stepped into their path, still wearing his cork shoes. Travis didn't hear him coming and slammed on his brakes. The crates of bottles in Travis' trailer all crashed and smashed together.

"I'm sorry, Farmer Pickles!" wailed Spud.

Bob was still collecting bark from the cork trees when Wendy telephoned to tell him about the broken bottles. "And there aren't any bottle tops left," she said.

"I might have just the thing – we can use the cork!" said Bob.

Bob and Muck drove straight to the factory. In no time, all the crates of bottles were corked and ready to deliver.

"Well done, Spud, for finding the cork trees," said Bob. Spud looked pleased.

Later, Bob hung the new cork lifebelt at the riverbank. The job was finished!

That night, Farmer Pickles told Spud he could stay at Scarecrow Cottage.

"I've made these special earplugs out of cork from your funny trees!" smiled Farmer Pickles. And with that, he put a cork in each ear and fell fast asleep!

Spud was delighted! "Ha-ha! Noisy Spud saved the day!" he laughed.